To Dad, Mom, Andy, and Stephanie.
Our love is small, but it is big, too.

And to Victoria Safford.
Your big and small words
inspired this big and small story.

Balzer + Bray is an imprint of HarperCollins Publishers.

Bigger Than a Bumblebee
Copyright © 2021 by Joseph Kuefler
All rights reserved. Manufactured in Italy.
No part of this book may be used or reproduced in any manner whatsoever without written permission except
in the case of brief quotations embodied in critical articles and reviews. For information address HarperCollins
Children's Books, a division of HarperCollins Publishers, 195 Broadway, New York, NY 10007.
www.harpercollinschildrens.com

ISBN 978-0-06-269165-1

Typography by Dana Fritts and Joseph Kuefler
21 22 23 24 25 RTLO 10 9 8 7 6 5 4 3 2 1
❖
First Edition

BIGGER
Than a
BUMBLEBEE

By
JOSEPH KUEFLER

Balzer + Bray
An Imprint of HarperCollinsPublishers

My little darling,
you are so big.

You are bigger than
the dandelions rising

and the caterpillars
climbing

and the busy bees
bumbling from one flower
to the next.

You are bigger than
the croaking toad

and the dragonflies dancing

and the timid turtle
taking its time.

You are bigger than
the nesting birds

and the quiet desert hare

and the tumbleweed
traveling this way
and that.

You are bigger than

him

and her

and this

and that

and these

and them

and so many other things.

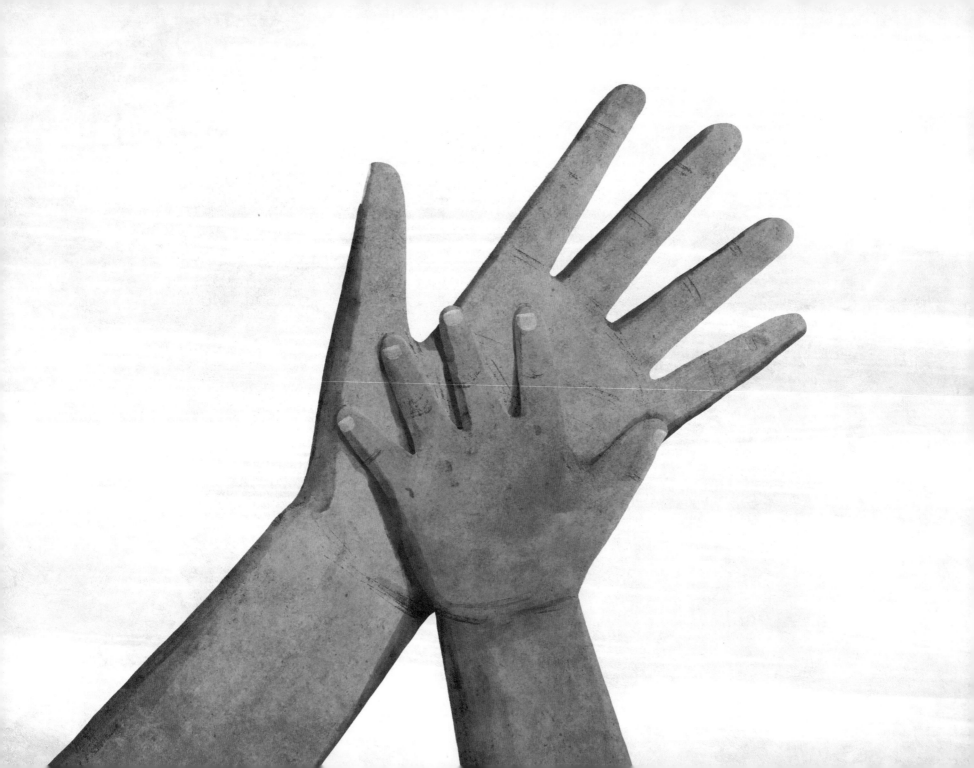

You are big.

But you are small, too.

You are smaller than
the brown bear fishing

and the waterfall flowing

and the granite rocks
growing moss on their sides.

You are smaller than
the wildebeests racing

and the wild lion chasing

and the sun-soaked savanna
stretching farther than forever.

You are smaller than
the icebergs breaking

and the northern lights shining

and the ocean tides
that rise and fall
and rise again.

You are smaller than him

and her

and these two.

And so many other things.

You are smaller than
the turning planets

and the bright-burning stars

and every galaxy
that was and is and will ever be.

You are smaller than love.

Love is a sheltering hug.

Love is a tender kiss.

Love is them

and this

and these two

and so many other things.

Most of all, my darling,
love is me and you.

Our love is small,
but it is big, too.